The Adventures of
MARY-KATE & ASHLEY ™

The Case Of The
Sea World ®
Adventure ™

The Case Of The
Sea World.
Adventure™

A novelization by Cathy East Dubowski

DUALSTAR PUBLICATIONS   PARACHUTE PRESS, INC.

SCHOLASTIC INC.

New York   Toronto   London   Auckland   Sydney

DUALSTAR PUBLICATIONS ™ PARACHUTE PRESS, INC

Dualstar Publications
c/o 1801 Century Park East
Los Angeles, CA 90067

Parachute Press, Inc.
156 Fifth Avenue
Suite 325
New York, NY 10010

Published by Scholastic Inc.

With special thanks to Robert Thorne and Harold Weitzberg.

Printed in the U.S.A.
April 1996
ISBN: 0-590-86369-X
I J

Ready for Adventure?

It was the best of times, it was the worst of times. Actually, it was bedtime when our great-grandmother would read us stories of mystery and suspense. It was then that we decided to be detectives.

The story you are about to read is one of the cases from the files of the Olsen and Olsen Mystery Agency. We call it *The Case Of The Sea World Adventure*.

Ashley and I were at Sea World with Mom and Dad. We were itching for an adventure. And we found one—when a mysterious person disappeared into thin air!

The chase was on! The Trenchcoat Twins were hot on the trail of a very scary lady dressed in black. But we weren't worried.

We always live up to our motto: Will Solve Any Crime By Dinner Time!

Chapter 1

Hi! My name is Mary-Kate Olsen. My twin sister, Ashley, and I are the Trenchcoat Twins. What do we do? We solve crimes. We love mysteries! We're detectives!

We have a silent partner—our dog, Clue. She's a brown and white bloodhound. She has floppy ears and a big wet nose. Our great-grandmother Olive gave us Clue the summer we spent on her farm. Great-grandma Olive loves mysteries, too. She thought a dog like Clue would be a big help in sniffing out clues.

We usually do our detective work in our office. It's in the attic of our house in

California. We have an ordinary-sized house in an ordinary-sized neighborhood.

Our family is ordinary size, too. Besides Ashley and me (and Clue) there's our Mom and Dad, our little sister, Lizzie, who's six, and our big brother, Trent. He's eleven.

I guess the only thing about us that *isn't* ordinary is the fact that Ashley and I are twins. Which sometimes drives us both crazy. But more about that later.

Right now we're someplace that isn't at all ordinary. We're at Sea World of Florida. Sea World is a really cool place. It's a marine-life park filled with birds, dolphins, whales, fish, turtles—everything.

"I love Sea World," Ashley said as we hurried through the park. It was a bright, sunny morning. "I love working here."

"Get real. We're *not* working!" I told her. "There's not a mystery in sight."

"If only we could talk to the animals,"

Ashley said. "Maybe they could find us a case we could crack."

I stopped in front of the parrots' cage. I whipped out my detective's notebook. (I keep the notebook with me at all times. Great-grandma Olive told me to do that. She says a good detective is always ready for a good mystery.)

I stood face-to-face with a parrot. I held my pen ready to write—name, address, reasons to suspect a crime.

"Give us the facts," I told the parrot. "And don't hold back."

"Yeah," Ashley added. "We have ways to make you squawk!"

The parrot blinked. "Bwwaack!" it said.

Ashley and I giggled. We couldn't *really* talk to the animals at Sea World. But our parents could—almost.

Mom and Dad are computer geniuses. They are trying to figure out how people can use computers to communicate with dolphins.

Dad knows everything about computers. And Mom knows everything Dad *doesn't* know!

Mom and Dad work together. Usually they work at home. But they also travel wherever they are needed. Ashley and I thought their job at Sea World was the best one yet—because *we* got to come along!

A big place like Sea World is sure to have at least one important mystery to solve.

Bong! A bell tower chimed in the distance.

"Come on, Ashley," I cried. "It's time to open our detective stand."

Ashley, Clue, and I raced over to a stand in the middle of the park.

A detective stand. Our detective stand. Dad helped us make it when we came to Sea World. Across the top of the stand was a big sign that read:

MARY-KATE & ASHLEY—DETECTIVES
WILL SOLVE ANY CRIME
BY DINNER TIME

But no one was waiting at our stand. Not one customer!

We were itching for a case—with nowhere to scratch.

"I know how to solve our problem," Ashley said. "It's totally logical."

I stared at my sister. Sometimes it's really hard to believe we're twins. We're both nine years old. We both have strawberry blond hair and big blue eyes. We both look exactly alike.

But we sure don't act alike. Or even think alike!

Ashley takes her time with everything. She thinks and thinks about every problem. And then she thinks some more. She studies every possible clue before she makes a move. Then when she does move, it's very, very slowly.

Not me. I always want to jump right in!

Ashley stared right back at me. "Mary-Kate, don't you want to know the reason why we have no case to solve?"

I sighed. "Okay, Ashley. Why don't we have a case to solve?"

"Because we're at Sea World. Everyone comes to Sea World to have fun. Not to hire detectives!" she said.

"Maybe you're right," I answered. "But I'm sick of waiting for a mystery. We need a case. And fast!"

Chapter 2

Just then two guys ran up to the stand. They were dressed like clowns. They started turning cartwheels and somersaults.

"Bobo and Flippy—you aren't helping!" Ashley told them. "You're always fooling around in front of our detective stand!"

We know Bobo and Flippy well. They are always hanging out at Sea World. They make us laugh. They make *everyone* laugh.

Bobo and Flippy wear black pants and shirts, black hats, and white cotton gloves. Their faces are covered in white face paint. They don't talk at all. Instead they act out everything they need to say.

We like Bobo and Flippy a lot. But sometimes they act so silly that nobody comes
near our detective stand.

"Shoo!" I yelled at them. "Go away!"

But they didn't go.

Flippy ran right up to a lady who was
passing by. He plucked a huge wad of bub-
ble gum right out of her mouth! She giggled
and walked away.

"Why did Flippy do that?" I asked.

Before Ashley could answer, Bobo yanked
off one of his floppy black shoes. He threw
the shoe to Flippy. Flippy caught it. He stuck
the wad of gum onto the bottom of Bobo's
shoe. He hugged and kissed the shoe.

"You love a shoe?" Ashley guessed.

"With gum on it?" I added.

"You love gumshoes!" We both groaned.

In case you didn't know, gumshoe is
another name for detective.

"That's funny, guys," I told them. "But

you're chasing away our customers."

"Mary-Kate is right," Ashley agreed. "You guys are bad for business!"

Bobo and Flippy wiped at their eyes. They pretended to cry.

"Uh-oh," I said. "I think we really hurt their feelings."

"We're sorry," I apologized.

"We didn't mean to chase you away," Ashley added. "We think you're very funny. But right now we need a mystery!"

Bobo and Flippy grinned. They leaped up in the air and spun around in circles. When they landed, they ran up to a chubby man wearing a suit and tie and spun him around, too.

"That's Mr. Kramer!" I gasped. "Put him down, clowns!"

"You can't treat the manager of Sea World like that," Ashley scolded. "He might get really mad!"

Bobo and Flippy put Mr. Kramer down. Mr. Kramer stroked his thick mustache and laughed.

"Woof! Woof!" Clue added.

"I don't mind," Mr. Kramer said. "I'm used to them. Now go away, Bobo and Flippy!" he said, smiling. "Let the twin detectives get to work."

Bobo and Flippy waved good-bye to us and skipped off.

"Solve any crimes today?" Mr. Kramer asked us.

"Not yet, Mr. Kramer," Ashley reported.

"You run Sea World," I said. "Isn't there a way *you* could hire us? We're really good detectives."

Mr. Kramer smiled. "I would hire you two in a minute. *If* I had a mystery to solve."

"There must be a mystery somewhere around here," I said.

Mr. Kramer shrugged. "You never know!"

He bent down and scratched Clue behind the ears. Then he strolled away.

"Hmmm." Ashley frowned. "I guess there's nothing we can do. We'll just have to wait for a mystery to happen."

"I don't want to wait," I grumbled. "We need a mystery now. And I'm going to find one!"

I stomped off. Ashley followed me. So did Clue. And we ran right into Bobo and Flippy!

Bobo jumped up and down and pointed at his wrist. He seemed upset. Flippy jerked his arms in a circle.

"They're trying to tell us something," Ashley said.

"Yeah," I agreed. "And I have a hunch it's *not* something good."

Bong! Bong! A bell tower chimed in the distance.

Bobo and Flippy grew more upset.

"Oh, no!" I shrieked.

Suddenly I knew what they were trying to tell us! And it definitely was *not* something good.

Chapter 3

"Ashley, we're late!" I said, tugging on my sister's arm.

"It's already two o'clock!" Ashley said. "We're supposed to meet Mom and Dad at Dolphin Stadium—like now!"

Mom and Dad were working in the show as part of their project at Sea World. And we were going to sing in it. The dolphin show is a big part of their computer project. Now we were going to ruin it!

Ashley and I raced over to the stadium. It was really crowded—packed as tight as a can of sardines. Everyone was waiting for our big number.

"And now, ladies and gentlemen, boys and girls! Joining us for the grand finale—a couple of birds who always go formal!"

That was Dad. He was introducing us to the audience. But we weren't ready yet. We heard the music to our song blaring over the loudspeakers.

"Hurry up, Mary-Kate!" Ashley said. "We still have to get into our costumes!"

Ashley and I ran backstage. We squirmed into our furry, black and white penguin suits. I jammed on the penguin head and started for the door.

"Wait a minute!" Ashley said. "Your head's on crooked!"

"Who cares?" I said. "So I'll be a penguin with a crooked neck!"

We waddled onto the stage as fast as we could. It's not easy to run with webbed feet!

The audience clapped and whistled when they saw us. We stood at the edge of the dolphins' pool. We had to catch our breath!

Dad typed a command into his computer: *Dolphins, take Mom for a ride!*

The dolphins heard the signal. They swam underwater near the edge of the pool. Mom leaped into the water. While she was under the water, she placed one foot on each of the dolphins. The dolphins swam to the top of the water—and Mom was standing on their backs.

Everyone cheered.

Dolphins—stop! Dad typed.

The dolphins turned and swam back to the edge of the pool. Mom jumped off just as our music began again.

"Time to sing!" I told Ashley. "We made it just in time!"

Here's our song:

"I picked you out from twenty million birds.

Instant friends! It only took four words.
I said, 'Yo!'
You said, 'Whoa!'
I said, 'Play?'
You said, 'Hey!'
And so began a splendid partnership.
And when I think about it, I flip!
FLIP!"

Every time we sang "Flip!" the dolphins flipped in the air. It was so cool! The audience clapped and cheered even louder.

Dolphins—dive! Dad typed into his computer.

The dolphins flew through the air and dived back into the pool. The show ended with a super-big dolphin SPLASH!

Ashley jabbed me in the ribs. "Don't forget to bow!"

"Don't worry," I told her. I couldn't *stop* bowing. I love being onstage. Mom always says that I'm a natural actress. I even tried to do a curtsy in my penguin costume. The audience cheered louder. So I curtsied again.

"Enough, Mary-Kate," Ashley finally said. "Mom and Dad are waiting for us."

I bowed two more times. Ashley and I ran offstage. I was grinning from ear to ear. But my grin faded when I saw Mom and Dad. They were definitely not clapping. Or even smiling.

Uh-oh. "Be smart. Act cool," I whispered to Ashley.

"No problem!" Ashley whispered back.

We flashed our parents our most charming smiles.

"Hi, sweet, wonderful, adoring parents!" we said together.

Ashley grabbed my wing. "Well, we have to go!" she said.

"Just a minute, you two," Dad said. "You wandered off without telling us where you were going. You almost missed the show!"

"Guilty," I said.

"*With* an explanation!" Ashley added.

"No explanations," Mom said. "Your detective business is fine—as long as it doesn't get in the way of your responsibilities. Working in this show is a big responsibility."

"I have a hunch," I whispered to Ashley. "I think we're about to be punished."

"You'll have to be punished," Mom said.

"Told you," I whispered to Ashley.

"I've called a baby-sitter," Mom went on.

"Not a baby-sitter!" I hollered.

"That's not logical," Ashley said. "We're detectives—not babies."

But Mom and Dad had made up their minds. We were done for.

Chapter 4

Our punishment was worse than I thought.

"It's Mrs. Torres!" Ashley groaned. We sat side by side on the couch in our apartment at Sea World. We stared at our babysitter.

"I'd rather have Bobo and Flippy baby-sit," I whispered back. "At least they never talk."

Mrs. Torres talked all the time. She was the worst baby-sitter. She loved to tell long stories that were always all mixed up.

"I like our baby-sitters back home," Ashley said.

I agreed. At home one of our neighbors sat for all of us.

"Trent and Lizzie are so lucky," Ashley said.

True. Trent was away at summer camp. Lizzie was visiting our grandparents for a few weeks. They *were* lucky. They didn't need any baby-sitters.

Mom and Dad loved Mrs. Torres. They met her at the Sea World lost-and-found office. They thought she was a real find. We wished she'd get lost.

"Now, both of you listen to Mrs. Torres," Mom told us. "She'll stay with you the rest of the afternoon."

Mom and Dad were getting ready to go back to work.

"But Mom," I said in my sweetest voice. "Why don't we stay with you?"

"Yes," Ashley added. "You're better than any baby-sitter."

"Sorry, kids. It's already been settled. I have to go to work," Mom said as she and

Dad hurried out the door of our apartment.

"Be good!" Dad called as he closed the door.

Mrs. Torres giggled. "Okay, sweeties!" she squealed. "Why don't I tell you my very most favorite story? 'The Three Bears!'"

Ashley and I groaned.

"Once upon a time," Mrs. Torres began, "a girl named Little Red Cinderella went to the Three Bears' house. Guess what she found? A *huge* beanstalk! A cute guy was swinging on it. He was shouting like this: Ah-ah-ah-ah-ah!" Mrs. Torres beat her chest as if she were Tarzan.

She was getting everything mixed up—as usual! We had to sneak away.

I poked Ashley in the ribs. "Come on!" I whispered. "We're busting out of this joint!"

"Do you think we should?" Ashley said. "I don't know. Maybe we'd better wait and think this through."

I shook my head. As I said before, sometimes Ashley spends too much time thinking about things. Lucky for her, she has me to make up her mind!

Mrs. Torres was still talking. "Little Red Cinderella screamed," she said. Then she let out a loud yell. Clue whimpered.

"I'm leaving—now!" I whispered. "And so are you."

"All right," Ashley said. "But remember, this was your idea."

I grinned. The Trenchcoat Twins always stick together!

"We'll sneak out the back door," I told Ashley. "Wait till Mrs. Torres is looking the other way. We'll make a break for it."

Mrs. Torres was still caught up in her story. "Then Jack swung on the beanstalk," she said. Mrs. Torres whirled around, with her back turned to us.

"Now!" I whispered.

Ashley and I jumped up. We ducked behind the couch.

"The giant chased after Jack," Mrs. Torres said. She slashed an imaginary sword through the air. "Give back that glass slipper!" Mrs. Torres was really into her story.

Ashley and I tiptoed toward the back door. Clue crept after us. I held my breath and turned the doorknob. The door swung open. It didn't make a sound.

Yes! We hurried outside. Mrs. Torres didn't even notice that we were gone.

Olsen and Olsen were back on the case. Except that we didn't have a case.

We hurried through Sea World. Clue kept up with us.

"Let's check back at our stand," I told Ashley.

"Wait!" Ashley stopped and pointed across a pond filled with pink flamingos. "Look,

Mary-Kate. There are Mom and Dad. Over there. Right behind the flamingo pool."

Uh-oh! We ducked behind a park bench.

Our parents were talking with Mr. Kramer.

"That's weird," Ashley said. "They're all frowning. I wonder if something is wrong?"

"We'd better listen," I told her.

Lucky for us we'd brought along our Super-Duper Snoop-a-Phone. It's a great detective tool. Dad helped us make it. It has pink headphones that fit over our ears. The headphones are hooked up to a big metal funnel.

Ashley and I slipped on the headphones. We aimed the funnel at the grown-ups and listened carefully.

Mr. Kramer shook his head. "We're old friends," he told Mom and Dad. "And I'm glad the dolphin program is going so well. But you haven't taken a vacation in years!"

Mom folded her arms. "We know we're

working hard," she began.

"But the dolphin program is almost finished," Dad added.

"I know," Mr. Kramer said. "But you really need a vacation. I used to be just like you. All work and no play. Then, before I knew it, my two sons were all grown up. I was sorry that I didn't spend more time with them when they were young."

Mom laughed. "We're not going to wait *that* long to take a vacation," she promised.

"Of course not," Dad said. "I've just got to work out a few more kinks in the program—"

Mr. Kramer stroked his mustache. "I wish I could make you change your minds."

I clicked off our Super-Duper Snoop-a-Phone. Ashley and I looked at each other and sighed. We heard every word loud and clear. Now we wished we hadn't!

"Poor Mom and Dad. No vacation—again," Ashley said.

"I know," I said. "They're always working. We're having fun here at Sea World. But all they do is work."

"Maybe there's something we can do for them," Ashley said.

"Maybe," I said. "But they like working on the dolphin program. Our problem is—we still haven't found a mystery. Come on, let's keep looking. I have a hunch we're about to stumble on something big."

Ashley rolled her eyes. "You and your hunches!"

Chapter 5

Ashley and I decided to bike through the park. Ashley's bike is pink. And she wears a pink helmet. My bike is lavender. I wear a light blue helmet. We both have nameplates on the backs of our bikes.

Mine says CRIME. And Ashley's nameplate says STOPPERS.

CRIME STOPPERS.

We decided we were going to search everywhere in Sea World for a mystery. But we couldn't go too fast because Clue was still with us. Clue is a super-duper sniffer-outer. But she is a little slow. Still, it always helps to have her along.

"If only somebody would *start* a crime—" Ashley began.

"Then we could stop it!" I finished.

Ashley slammed on her brakes. Her bike tires squealed on the sidewalk. "I see a crime! Look over there."

"What? Where?" I braked to a stop. My heart was pounding.

"There!" Ashley pointed into the woods. "Littering!"

"Littering? You mean throwing garbage on the ground?" I shook my head. "That's not much of a crime, Ashley."

"But it *is* a crime," Ashley argued. "And solving a litter mystery is more interesting than listening to Mrs. Torres all day."

"True," I agreed.

We dropped our bikes at the edge of the sidewalk, near a stone wall.

Clue barked loudly as we hurried into the woods.

It was cool and quiet under the trees. Branches spread overhead like a leafy green tent. In front of us stood a small wooden footbridge.

A heap of litter was lying on the other side of the bridge. Both of us stared at it.

"Wait a minute," I said. "That's not litter."

Ashley and I slowly crept closer.

"It looks like a person," Ashley said.

"You're right," I told her. "A person lying in a heap. And covered with leaves!"

We looked at each other.

"What is a person doing lying in the woods?" I wondered aloud.

Ashley shrugged. "I don't know," she said. "It's a mystery to me."

A mystery?

"Yes!" I shouted. My hunch was right! We found a mystery.

Ashley and I slapped a high five. We ran across the footbridge for a closer look.

The person lay facedown in the leaves. He was tall and thin. He wore a light tan raincoat and dark pants and shoes. A tan hat with a wide, floppy brim lay on the ground next to him.

I whipped out my detective's notebook.

Ashley pulled out her magnifying glass.

"Ready to begin, Detective Olsen?" Ashley asked.

"Ready, Detective Olsen," I answered.

"Ready, Clue?" we asked our partner.

"Woof!" Clue barked in reply.

We stepped closer to the mystery person.

Clue sniffed while I made notes. CRIME SCENE: The woods. WHERE: Right over the footbridge. CLUES: One tall, thin man in tan. NAME: Don't know.

"See if you can find out his name," I told Ashley.

"Hello," she called out.

No answer.

"Hey, mister!" I called loudly.

Still no answer.

I leaned down and shouted, "WAKE UP!"

He didn't move an inch.

"Uh, Ashley," I said. "I don't think he's breathing."

"Maybe he's sleeping," Ashley said. "And holding his breath."

"When he's sleeping?" I asked.

Ashley's eyes grew wide. "I guess he's . . . NOT SLEEPING!"

That could mean only one thing.

Ashley and I stared at each other. "AAAG-GHHHH!" we both started screaming. Clue let out a loud howl.

We ran as fast as we could over the foot-bridge.

"Where are we going?" I asked.

"To get Officer Friendly!" Ashley climbed on her bike. "He'll know what to do."

"You wait here, Clue," I said.

I hopped on my bike and sped after Ashley.

A few minutes later we arrived at Officer Friendly's tiny office. It was right near the main entrance to the park. Officer Friendly had a very important job. He kept the park safe for visitors.

Ashley and I burst into his office.

"Officer Friendly," I called. "We need your help!"

"It's really important," Ashley added.

Both of us started to talk at once. Somehow we managed to tell him all about our mystery.

"An unknown person is lying in the woods at Sea World?" Officer Friendly shook his head. "I find that hard to believe."

"It's true," Ashley insisted.

I showed Officer Friendly my detective's notebook. "I wrote down all our clues here," I told him. I read out loud from my notes.

"One tall, thin man in tan."

"You'd better come and check it out for yourself," Ashley said.

"Okay," Officer Friendly said. "But this better not take too long." He climbed into his little white cart. We jumped onto our bikes. We led Officer Friendly to the scene of the crime.

"This way!" Ashley shouted. She skidded to a stop next to the stone wall.

"He's over there in the woods," I said. I dropped my bike on the pavement. Officer Friendly parked his white cart. Clue barked in excitement. She ran ahead of us across the footbridge.

Leaves crunched beneath our feet as we ran after Clue. Officer Friendly had a hard time keeping up with us.

"Slow down, girls!" Officer Friendly called.

Ashley and I crossed the footbridge.

We stared at the ground.

All we saw was a pile of leaves.
Nobody was there.
The Man in Tan was gone!

We're Mary-Kate and Ashley—the Trenchcoat Twins. With the help of our dog Clue, we love to solve mysteries!

Ashley and I set up a detective stand at Sea World— but no one brought us a crime to solve!

Bobo and Flippy—two clowns—were the only people to stop by our stand.

Mr. Kramer, the manager of Sea World, told us not to worry—a mystery would come along for sure.

We decided to have some fun. We dressed up as penguins and sang in a water show!

But we still had no mystery to solve. How could we find one if we were stuck at home with the baby-sitter? That's when we escaped!

The search for a case to crack continued!

A-ha! A crime! Ashley and I found a mysterious body in the woods!

We ran for help. But when we returned...

...the body was gone!

Then we spotted a Lady in Black carrying the body!

And we found a clue: A note that said the Lady in Black was headed for the pier!

We didn't have any money to hire a taxi to the pier. So we teamed up with a street band to make some quick cash!

We arrived at the pier just in time to follow the Lady in Black on board!

The Lady in Black was Bobo!

But what was Bobo doing there? Ashley and I figured it out—can you?

Chapter 6

"I knew it," Officer Friendly said. "There's nobody here."

"He *was* right here," Ashley insisted. "We both saw him, plain as day. Right, Mary-Kate?"

"Right," I agreed.

But nobody was there now.

Officer Friendly had that look on his face. The look that grown-ups get when they *pretend* they believe you—but they really don't.

"Well, that's what always happens to a mystery body," Officer Friendly said with a chuckle. "It gets up and walks away as soon as you turn your back." He glanced at his watch. "Okay, you two, have fun. I need to get back to work."

Officer Friendly led Ashley and me out of the woods. He climbed into his cart and drove away.

"Great." I sighed. "Our mystery person has turned into a *missing* person. Officer Friendly doesn't believe us. Now no one will believe us."

I shook my head. We had a real mystery—and we let it get away. I didn't know what to do next.

Ashley plopped down on the stone wall. She twisted a lock of hair around her finger. That meant she was thinking. Thinking hard.

"This isn't logical," she announced. "Somebody must have moved him. But who?" she asked. "And why?"

"I don't know. But we're going to find out." I jumped to my feet. "Let's get on the case right away, Detective."

"Wait," Ashley said. "The first thing to do is search the scene of the crime."

"Good idea, Ashley. Great-grandma Olive would be proud. Let's go!" I whistled for Clue. "Okay, girl. Time to put your super-duper sniffer to work."

Clue shoved her nose into the pile of leaves. She pawed the ground and barked.

"Look!" Ashley said. "She found something!"

Good old Clue!

We both bent down to see what it was.

"It's a wallet," Ashley said. She held up a black leather wallet. It looked like a man's wallet. "We'd better turn this in to the lost-and-found."

I snatched the wallet away from her. "Not yet. This is a great clue! A very important clue. Let's look inside."

I opened the wallet very carefully.

"There's a picture in here," I said. Then I groaned. "A *weird* picture. It only shows the *back* of someone's head."

I gave the photo to Ashley. She stared at it and grinned. "I know who this is!" she said.

"Who? Who?" I asked.

"It's our missing person. I'd know the back of his head anywhere," she explained.

"This proves he was here," I said. "Anything else?"

"Yes," she said. "Here are two tickets to the Sea World Sky Tower."

The Sky Tower is a tall, thin building that stands in the middle of Sea World. It has a huge room at the top with windows all around. Through the windows you can see everything in the park—the animals, the visitors, Dolphin Stadium, and all the other buildings.

"Maybe we'll find our missing person there," Ashley added. "Or another clue."

"Great! I love the Sky Tower," I said. "Let's go."

We ran for our bikes.

A few minutes later we were in the Sky Tower, up in the clouds. We searched the big room. No sign of the Man in Tan.

We walked over to one of the big windows. Ashley pulled out a pair of binoculars from her backpack. Now she could see everything far away as if it were right up close.

"Mary-Kate!" Ashley exclaimed. "Take a look. See that lady with blond hair? She's driving a white cart just like Officer Friendly's. She's wearing a big black hat and a black coat."

"I see her. What's so special about her?" I asked.

"Look at the man who's in the cart. The one sitting next to her. See what he's wearing?" Ashley asked.

I gasped. "A tan raincoat. And a big tan hat with a wide, floppy brim."

"It's the Man in Tan!" we both shouted.

Chapter 7

"Are you sure it's really him?" I asked.

I pulled my binoculars out of my backpack and stared through them. Sure enough, the man in the cart was wearing the same tan raincoat we'd seen in the woods. On his head was the floppy, wide-brimmed hat we'd seen lying in the leaves. The hat was pulled down low to hide his face.

"Hmmm," Ashley said. She peered through her binoculars again. "Very interesting. He's *dressed* like the Man in Tan. But this person is sitting up."

The cart hit a bump and the man in the raincoat flopped around like crazy. In fact, he almost fell out of the cart. But the Lady in Black yanked him inside.

"A-ha!" Ashley exclaimed. "He's not *sitting* up. He's *propped* up. I conclude the only logical explanation. It *is* our missing person. See?"

"Yeah. And I see something else, too!" I turned to Ashley. "The Lady in Black is driving toward the gate. I've got a hunch. She's trying to sneak out of the park. We've got to stop her!"

The chase was on!

The good news was we finally had a real case. It had everything: Real clues. A real suspect. A real missing person. It even had a real chase!

The bad news was our missing person was getting away. Again!

We raced out of the Sky Tower with Clue right behind us. We ran smack into the middle of a huge crowd of people. They were busy walking around taking pictures. And they were blocking the sidewalk.

"Excuse us. Excuse us, please!" Ashley tried to get through the crowd.

"Woof! Woof!" Clue barked.

No one paid attention.

"Everyone say 'cheese,'" I shouted.

The whole group of people stopped and stood frozen in place. "Cheese!" they all yelled at once, smiling.

I saw a clear path right between them.

"This way, Ashley!" I grabbed her hand and pulled her through the crowd. We ran past the crowd to the right.

"Hurry!" Ashley cried.

"I'm hurrying," I shouted to Ashley. "Don't let them out of your sight!"

Clue did her best to keep up with us. We headed for our bikes.

"Ashley! Look! Here comes the Lady in Black," I said.

The little white cart sped around the corner in front of us and drove out of sight.

"No time for bikes!" I shouted. "Let's run!"

Ashley and I chased the cart. It was hard running that fast, but we had to catch up. Clue was right on our heels.

The Lady in Black drove to the gate and parked the cart. She lifted the man out and placed her arm around his waist.

I whipped out my notebook and scribbled furiously. "Did you see that?" I asked Ashley.

"Yes. Our suspect is pretending that our missing person is a living, breathing guy," Ashley exclaimed.

"And she's getting away with it, too," I added.

I glanced around. No one else seemed to notice that anything strange was happening.

Not even Officer Friendly. He was standing at the gate, smiling and waving good-bye to all the people.

The Lady in Black carried the missing person past Officer Friendly. She went right through the gate.

"Come back again," Officer Friendly said. She nodded and hurried away.

I couldn't believe it. "A criminal is escaping—right under his nose!"

Ashley and I ran to the gate.

"Hello, girls," Officer Friendly said. "Still chasing after your missing person?" he teased.

"Yes. And there he is!" I said.

"Sure, sure." Officer Friendly winked at us.

He was no help. I turned to Ashley. "It's up to us—the Trenchcoat Twins. Come on." I pushed through the exit gate.

"Wait!" Ashley ran through the gate after me. She grabbed my arm. "We have a problem. A big problem. We can't follow them."

"Why not?" I asked.

"Because." Ashley took a deep breath. "We're not allowed to leave Sea World by ourselves," she said.

She was right. I stared down the street.

The Lady in Black was getting away!

Chapter 8

We had to make a choice. Fast.

"We can't let our suspect escape," I said. "I vote to chase them now and think about it later."

Ashley hesitated. "There is some logic to that," she said. "If we don't move now, we might lose their trail."

Ashley turned to Clue. "Go home, Clue. Tell Mom and Dad we're on a case. We'll be home by dinner time."

We watched Clue run off.

"Let's go," I said. I grabbed Ashley's arm and pulled her across the street.

"Don't forget to look both ways," Ashley

told me for the zillionth time in our lives.

"Don't worry," I said. "We can be safe *and* brave—at the same time."

We followed the Lady in Black to a parking lot right outside Sea World. The Lady in Black glanced our way.

"Mary-Kate! Get down!" Ashley pulled me behind some bushes.

The lady looked around the parking lot. She made sure no one was watching her. Then she carried our missing person to a beat-up red van. The van was painted with flowers, smiling faces, and two white-gloved hands. She opened the door of the van and took out a big blue duffel bag. She pushed and shoved the Man in Tan into the bag. Then she shoved the bag inside the van.

The Lady in Black jumped into the driver's seat and drove away.

I whipped out my notebook and quickly wrote: SUSPECT: The Lady in Black. ACTIONS:

Stuffed Man in Tan into big blue duffel bag.

"She dropped something!" Ashley yelled.

"Another clue!" I dashed across the parking lot—being careful to look both ways. I found the clue and picked it up.

"What is it?" Ashley asked.

"It's an ad for a holiday cruise ship," I said. "You know, like those great big boats we see on TV sometimes? Wow. Just look at these pictures! This ship has a swimming pool, great food, and all kinds of games." I turned the ad over. "Someone wrote something on the back."

"Let me see that," Ashley said. She pulled her magnifying glass out of her backpack and studied the handwriting. "Uh-oh," she said. "It looks like the Lady in Black is definitely taking this ship."

Ashley showed me the writing. It said, *Don't miss the boat!*

"If the Lady in Black gets on that ship,

we'll never catch her," Ashley said.

"Don't worry," I told her. I pointed to the ad. "See? It says right here—the ship doesn't leave until the tenth."

Ashley rolled her eyes. "Mary-Kate! Today *is* the tenth!"

"Well, it's still okay," I said. "The boat doesn't sail until four o'clock."

"But Mary-Kate!" Ashley said. "It's almost four o'clock now!"

Gulp!

"Looks like we're out of luck," I told my sister. "Because it also says that the ship leaves from the Port of Miami."

"Port of Miami? That's far away," Ashley said. "We could never get there on our bikes. Not by four o'clock."

"But we can make it—if we take a cab," I said. I ran to the curb and waved my hand in the air. "Taxi!" I shouted.

A yellow taxi pulled up to the curb. I

yanked open the door while Ashley counted our money.

"We need to get to the Port of Miami," I told the driver.

"How far can we go on twenty-eight cents?" Ashley asked.

The taxi driver laughed. "Across the street," he said. "And that's only if we make the green light. Sorry." He zoomed away.

"We need more money. And *fast*," I said.

Ashley frowned. "I don't even know how to get money *slow*."

Things were looking bad. But I had a hunch we were going to make that ship.

Suddenly I heard music. A group of street musicians was coming up the street, playing a lively song. People stopped to listen. And they dropped money into an open guitar case that the musicians placed on the sidewalk.

"Follow me, Ashley," I said. We walked

over to the group of musicians.

"Hi! My name is Mary-Kate and this is my sister, Ashley. We know how you could make twice as much money," I told the musicians. "Hire more singers. *Twin* singers. Us!"

The guitar player nodded. "Okay. That sounds like a good idea." He talked it over with the rest of his group.

"Let's do it," the drummer said.

"Here," the guitar player said. "Slip on these ruffled blouses over your T-shirts. Then you'll really look the part."

Ashley and I slipped the brightly colored shirts over our clothes.

"Ready, guys?" I shouted. "One, two, three—"

The musicians began to play. Ashley and I started to sing. More and more people gathered around. They clapped and danced and sang along. When the song was over, they dropped money into the guitar case.

"You girls can sing with us anytime," the drummer said. We returned the costumes he loaned us. He handed us our share of the money we'd earned.

"Thanks!" I said. "Port of Miami, here we come!"

Ashley counted the money. Her eyes lit up. "Wow! Ninety-eight dollars and fifteen cents. We can get *six* taxis!"

"Taxis?" I exclaimed. "Now we can afford to go in style!" I dashed to the nearest pay phone.

A few minutes later a shiny black limousine pulled up to the curb.

"Where to, ladies?" the driver asked.

Ashley slid into the fancy car. "Port of Miami!"

"And step on it!" I added, slamming the limousine door.

Chapter 9

"We should call home," Ashley said. "So Mom and Dad won't worry."

I nodded. "Good idea!" I reached for the car phone in the backseat of the limo. "I've always wanted to talk on one of these!"

"Better let me do the talking." Ashley grabbed the phone and dialed our apartment. "Oh, it's the answering machine!"

"Good," I said. "The answering machine can't yell at us. And we can still leave Mom and Dad a message to let them know that we're okay."

"Hi, Mom and Dad. This is Ashley—"

"And Mary-Kate."

"Clue is on her way home to tell you not to worry," Ashley said. "We wouldn't have left except—"

"We're on the case of the century!" I finished.

Ashley held the phone to one side. "Do you think we should tell them we're racing off in a limo to solve a crime? Should we tell them we're following a suspect to a ship docked at the Port of Miami?"

"Better not," I said. "Let's wait till we solve the case. Oops!" I covered my mouth. "I hope the machine didn't tape that!"

"Me too." Ashley held up the phone again. "Okay, Mom and Dad. We'll call back soon!" She hung up.

The limo swerved to a stop. "Here it is! Port of Miami," the driver called.

Ashley and I stepped out of the car. We stared at the enormous cruise ship that was docked in front of us.

"Wow! It's huge!" I exclaimed. "I wonder how many people it can hold? I wonder how fast it can go? I wonder—"

"I wonder if the Lady in Black is on that ship!" Ashley interrupted. "Let's investigate."

The dock was a busy place. Workers were loading boxes and crates onto the ship. Crowds of people were saying good-bye to their family and friends.

"There she is!" Ashley pointed at the gangplank—the walkway that led from the dock to the ship.

The Lady in Black struggled up the gangplank. She was dragging the big blue duffel bag behind her. A ship's officer in a white uniform checked her ticket. He smiled and let her go onboard.

"Follow that lady!" I shouted.

I started toward the ship.

"Wait, Mary-Kate!" Ashley grabbed my arm. "We don't have tickets. There's no way they'll ever let us on board that ship."

I looked around and spotted a stack of huge cardboard boxes near the dock. "I have an idea," I said. I whispered something to Ashley. She nodded.

We strolled over to the boxes. We found two empty ones and pulled them over our heads. The boxes covered us from head to toe. We poked holes in the front so we could see where we were going. Then we waited until the ship's officer looked the other way.

"Go!" I whispered.

Ashley and I scampered toward the ship. We looked like two walking boxes. The officer turned and stared in our direction.

"Freeze!" I whispered. Ashley and I stood still. I hoped we looked like two regular boxes.

If the officer noticed us, he would throw us off the ship. I held my breath. I didn't move. The officer took a step toward us.

Oh, no! He's coming this way, I thought.

But then he shrugged and went back to his work.

"Go!" I said.

We scooted all the way up the gangplank and onto the ship.

"Hey!" an officer behind us shouted. "Stop those boxes!"

Ashley and I raced down a long hallway and turned a corner. The officer ran past us and out of sight.

"Whoa! That was close!" I said. Ashley and I tossed off the boxes.

Thunk! A door opened. We heard footsteps coming our way.

"Quick! Over here!" Ashley said. We ducked out of sight.

It was the Lady in Black—with the blue duffel bag!

She headed down the hallway. Ashley and I followed right behind her.

"She went in there!" Ashley pointed to a door. We opened it and found ourselves in a storage room. We hid behind a stack of crates.

Ashley grabbed my hand. "Are you scared?"

"Not really," I said, squeezing Ashley's hand really tight.

"Are you lying?" Ashley asked.

I nodded. "Big time!"

Ker-thunk!

"What was that?" I cried.

Slowly we peeked over the crates. The Lady in Black was dragging the blue duffel bag toward an open window.

Ashley gasped. "She's going to throw the bag overboard!"

"We've got to stop her!" I turned and—

Bang! Crash!

I knocked over a stack of crates.

The Lady in Black dropped the bag and

whirled around. She stared right at us. Her eyes narrowed to an icy glare. She rushed at Ashley and me.

Double uh-oh!

Ashley and I grabbed on to each other. We were really in trouble now!

Chapter 10

"Hold it right there!" someone shouted.

The Lady in Black froze.

"Dad!" I yelled.

"Mom!" Ashley added.

Our parents raced into the storage room. We flew into their arms. Boy, were we glad to see them!

The ship's officer was right behind them.

"We were so worried!" Mom exclaimed.

"How did you know where to find us?" Ashley asked.

"The phone answering machine," Mom replied. "It recorded everything you girls said when you called us from the limo. Even the parts you *didn't* want us to hear. That's how we knew to look for you on the ship at the Port of Miami."

"Are you girls okay?" Dad asked.

"We're fine," Ashley said.

"Good!" Dad's smile turned into a scowl. "Now will somebody *please* tell me what this is all about?"

I pointed at the blue duffel bag. "There's a missing person in there. A Man in Tan."

"And *she* put him there!" Ashley added.

The Lady in Black was trying to sneak away. But the officer grabbed her before she could escape.

Dad marched over to the duffel bag. "Let's see what's really inside," he said.

He unzipped the bag. He pulled out a floppy tan hat.

"What in the world—!" Dad exclaimed, when he looked inside the bag.

Everyone gasped.

"Flippy?" I squealed.

The Man in Tan was Flippy the clown!

Flippy jumped up and gave Dad a big kiss on the cheek. Everybody laughed.

Dad walked up to the Lady in Black. "Then who are you?" he asked.

The Lady in Black turned away.

She pulled off her black hat. She pulled off her blond hair. It was a wig!

She turned around.

She was a *he*!

"Bobo!" Ashley exclaimed.

Bobo bowed and grinned.

I turned to my sister. "Are you thinking what I'm thinking?"

Ashley nodded. "You can come out now, Mr. Kramer!" we called.

Mr. Kramer popped out from behind some boxes. He had a huge grin on his face. He was wearing a brightly colored shirt and a straw hat. The kind of clothes that people wear when they're on vacation.

"You girls are A-one detectives," Mr. Kramer said. "How did you figure it out?"

"Simple deduction," Ashley answered. "We studied the evidence. And we figured there was something fishy about those two." She pointed at Bobo and Flippy.

Our parents still looked confused.

"Mr. Kramer couldn't get you to take a vacation," I explained to them. "But he knew you really needed one."

"And he knew we needed a big case," Ashley added.

"So he got Bobo and Flippy to fake a mystery. The Lady in Black stole the Man in Tan and brought him here. Mr. Kramer knew that we'd chase them."

"And he knew you would chase *us*," Ashley said. "He wanted to get all of us on this ship."

"But why?" Mom asked.

"Because we're going on a *cruise*!" I shouted. "On this ship!"

"That's right," Mr. Kramer said with a smile. "Courtesy of Sea World. A thank-you for all your hard work. I've already packed your clothes—and your computers!"

Mom and Dad were speechless.

"Dad," I said. "I know you're going to say no—"

"But don't!" Ashley begged.

Dad frowned. "I should be *furious*!"

Ashley and I closed our eyes and crossed our fingers.

"But I'm not," Dad added. "Mr. Kramer is right. We really *do* need a vacation. I was too stubborn to admit it. But now I say—let's do it!"

"All right!" Ashley and I jumped up and down in excitement.

I was so happy. A cruise! With our parents. I was already thinking of all the fun we could have together.

"And Bobo, Flippy, and I are all sailing with you," Mr. Kramer said.

"Oh, Jack, it's going to be so nice," Mom said to Dad. She gave him a big hug.

"Yeah," Dad agreed. "I'm really looking forward to a nice, quiet trip." Our parents strolled out of the room, holding hands. Bobo, Flippy, and Mr. Kramer walked after them.

Ashley shot me a horrified glance. "I hope this trip isn't too quiet," she said.

"Don't worry," I told her. "This is a big ship. And I have another hunch. I'll bet we find another mystery waiting for us onboard the ship—a mystery on the high seas!"

Hi—from both of us!

Did you like our Sea World Adventure? We had a great time working on that mystery. We solved the case and ended up going on an awesome vacation on a cruise ship! A cruise ship—can you believe it?

Mom and Dad told us all about cruise ships. Did you know that they have swimming pools, movie theaters, even a bowling alley right on the ship? Wow! We didn't!

And we didn't know something else—that there would be another cool mystery for us to solve there.

We hope you will read all about it in *The Case Of The Mystery Cruise*! In the meantime, if you have any questions, you can write us at:

MARY-KATE & ASHLEY'S FUN CLUB™
859 HOLLYWOOD WAY, SUITE 412
BURBANK, CA 91505

We would love to hear from you!

Love

Mary-Kate and Ashley

Mary-Kate & Ashley
Ready for Fun and Adventure? Read All Our Books!

THE NEW ADVENTURES OF MARY-KATE & ASHLEY™

- ❑ BBO-0-590-29542-X The Case of the Ballet Bandit $3
- ❑ BBO-0-590-29307-9 The Case of 202 Clues $3
- ❑ BBO-0-590-29305-5 The Case of the Blue-Ribbon Horse.................................$3
- ❑ BBO-0-590-29397-4 The Case of the Haunted Camp.....................................$3
- ❑ BBO-0-590-29401-6 The Case of the Wild Wolf River $3
- ❑ BBO-0-590-29402-4 The Case of the Rock & Roll Mystery.............................$3
- ❑ BBO-0-590-29404-0 The Case of the Missing Mummy $3
- ❑ BBO-0-590-29403-2 The Case of the Surprise Call $3
- ❑ BBO-0-439-06043-5 The Case of the Disappearing Princess............................$3

THE ADVENTURES OF MARY-KATE & ASHLEY™

- ❑ BBO-0-590-86369-X The Case of the Sea World™ Adventure $3
- ❑ BBO-0-590-86370-3 The Case of the Mystery Cruise......................................$3
- ❑ BBO-0-590-86231-6 The Case of the Funhouse Mystery $3
- ❑ BBO-0-590-88008-X The Case of the U.S. Space Camp™ Mission...................$3
- ❑ BBO-0-590-88009-8 The Case of the Christmas Caper $3
- ❑ BBO-0-590-88010-1 The Case of the Shark Encounter $3
- ❑ BBO-0-590-88013-6 The Case of the Hotel Who-Done-It $3
- ❑ BBO-0-590-88014-4 The Case of the Volcano Mystery $3
- ❑ BBO-0-590-88015-2 The Case of the U.S. Navy Adventure..............................$3
- ❑ BBO-0-590-88016-0 The Case of Thorn Mansion $3

YOU'RE INVITED TO MARY-KATE & ASHLEY'S™

- ❑ BBO-0-590-76958-8 You're Invited to Mary-Kate & Ashley's Christmas Party ....$12.
- ❑ BBO-0-590-88012-8 You're Invited to Mary-Kate & Ashley's Hawaiian Beach Party $12
- ❑ BBO-0-590-88007-1 You're Invited to Mary-Kate & Ashley's Sleepover Party $12
- ❑ BBO-0-590-22593-6 You're Invited to Mary-Kate & Ashley's Birthday Party $12
- ❑ BBO-0-590-29399-0 You're Invited to Mary-Kate & Ashley's Ballet Party...........................$12

- -

Available wherever you buy books, or use this order form
SCHOLASTIC INC., P.O. Box 7502, 2931 East McCarty Street, Jefferson City, MO 65102

Please send me the books I have checked above. I am enclosing $_____ (please add $2.00 to cover shipping and handling). Send check or money order—no cash or C.O.D.s please.

Name _____

Address_____

City_____ State/Zip _____

Please allow four to six weeks for delivery. Offer good in the U.S.A. only. Sorry, mail orders are not available to residents of Canada. Prices subject to change.

High Above Hollywood the Olsens Are Playing Matchmakers!

Check Them Out in Their Coolest New Movie

Mary-Kate Olsen **Ashley Olsen**

Billboard DAD

One's a surfer. The other's a high diver. When these two team up to find a new love for their single Dad by taking out a personals ad on a billboard in the heart of Hollywood, it's a fun-loving, eye-catching California adventure gone wild!

Now on Video!

DUALSTAR VIDEO

The party can't start without you...

YOU'RE INVITED TO MARY-KATE & ASHLEY'S

with a shiny dolphin necklace!

HAWAIIAN BEACH PARTY

BIRTHDAY PARTY

with a beautiful keepsake locket!

with a twin hearts necklace!

with a snowflake necklace!

Christmas Party

You've watched the videos, now read all the books! Order today!

❏ BCG93843-6	*You're Invited to Mary-Kate & Ashley's Sleepover Party*	$12.95
❏ BCG88012-8	*You're Invited to Mary-Kate & Ashley's Hawaiian Beach Party*	$12.95
❏ BCG76958-8	*You're Invited to Mary-Kate & Ashley's Christmas Party*	$12.95
❏ BCG22593-6	*You're Invited to Mary-Kate & Ashley's Birthday Party*	$12.95

Here's a message from Mary-Kate and Ashley...See you at the bookstore!

Available wherever you buy books, or use this order form

Scholastic Inc., P.O. Box 7502, 2931 East McCarty Street, Jefferson City, MO 65102

ase send me the books I have checked above. I am enclosing $_____ (please add $2.00 to cover shipping and ndling). Send check or money order—no cash or C.O.D.s please.

me_____ **Birthdate**_____

ldress_____

ty_____ **State/Zip** _____

ase allow four to six weeks for delivery. Offer good in
. only. Sorry, mail orders are not available to residents
Canada. Prices subject to change.

DUALSTAR PUBLICATIONS  PARACHUTE PRESS

CHOLASTIC

YIT298

Don't Miss

Mary-Kate & Ashley

in their 2 newest videos!

Costume Party

Mall Party

**Available Now
Only on Video.**

DUALSTAR VIDEO

It doesn't matter if you live around the corner...
or around the world...
If you are a fan of Mary-Kate and Ashley Olsen,
you should be a member of

MARY-KATE + ASHLEY'S FUN CLUB™

Here's what you get:
Our Funzine™
An autographed color photo
Two black & white individual photos
A full size color poster
An official **Fun Club**™ membership card
A **Fun Club**™ school folder
Two special **Fun Club**™ surprises
A holiday card
Fun Club™ collectibles catalog
Plus a **Fun Club**™ box to keep everything in

To join Mary-Kate + Ashley's Fun Club™, fill out the form
below and send it along with

U.S. Residents – $17.00
Canadian Residents – $22 U.S. Funds
International Residents – $27 U.S. Funds

MARY-KATE + ASHLEY'S FUN CLUB™
859 HOLLYWOOD WAY, SUITE 275
BURBANK, CA 91505

NAME:_____

ADDRESS:_____

CITY:_____STATE:_____ZIP:_____

PHONE: (____) _____BIRTHDATE:_____